For Em,
stylish and silly
in equal measure!

First American Edition 2021
Kane Miller, A Division of EDC Publishing

Text and illustrations copyright © Heath McKenzie, 2019.
Heath McKenzie asserts his moral rights as the author
and illustrator of this work.

First published by Scholastic Press, an imprint of
Scholastic Australia Pty Limited in 2019.
This edition published under license
of Scholastic Australia Pty Ltd.

For information contact:
Kane Miller, A Division of EDC Publishing
5402 S 122nd E Ave, Tulsa, OK 74146
www.kanemiller.com
www.myubam.com

Library of Congress Control Number: 2020938408

Printed and bound in China
3 4 5 6 7 8 9 10

ISBN: 978-1-68464-221-2

NOW THAT'S A HAT!

HEATH McKENZIE

Kane Miller
A DIVISION OF EDC PUBLISHING

GOOD MORNING!
I'd like to buy a **NEW HAT.**

Well, come right in, sir, I can help you with that.

I'm after an **EVERYDAY** kind of thing.
Something to wear
WINTER, SUMMER, or **SPRING.**

AHA! Something that suits every day of the week?
A handy "all-rounder," that's slightly unique?

Here's just the thing, from the *House of DeGrott*.

Hmmm... that's not bad...
but **WHAT ELSE** have you got?

No, this hat is too **TALL.**

This hat is too **SMALL.**

This hat is too **TALL** but is also too **SMALL!**

And this one's ALL WRONG.

This hat is too SHORT.

I feel that this hat
is a wee bit too

LONG.

This hat is too **LIVELY**.

This hat is too **DEAD.**

Are you sure this hat isn't an old
LOAF OF BREAD?

A bit too much **SPARKLE.**

A bit
too much
FRUIT.

I know that you know
this is really
A BOOT!

This hat is too **ROYAL.**

This hat is too **HOLEY.**

This hat has a little too much **GUACAMOLE!**

This hat is too **ROMAN.**

This hat is too **DUTCH.**

This hat
is maybe
a little

TOO MUCH?!

There's no need for **BICORNES, BERETS** or **CORK HATS, SOMBREROS** or **FEZZES** or even that **GAT!**

I don't want to wear
a **FAIRGROUND**
on my head.

There's no need for headwear that needs to be **FED!**

I just want a **PLAIN, BORING, EVERYDAY HAT!**

Surely somewhere you'd have one . . .

SQUAWK!

JUST LIKE THAT!!!!

Yes, it's perfect.
I'll take it!
I like that a lot!

What a fine
choice, sir.
And it's
the last one
I've got.

The **LAST ONE** in stock!
How lucky is that?!

GOOD MORNING,
I'd like to buy a **NEW HAT!**